For my parents, with thanks for a happy childhood —J.O.
For Liberty Bell —C.A.

Visit us on the Web! randomhouse.com/kids

Educators and librarians, for a variety of teaching tools, visit us at RHTeachersLibrarians.com

Library of Congress Cataloging-in-Publication Data
Offill, Jenny.
Sparky / by Jenny Offill ; illustrated by Chris Appelhans.—First edition.
pages cm
Summary: A child takes a sloth named Sparky as a pet.
ISBN 978-0-375-87023-1 (trade) — ISBN 978-0-375-97023-8 (glb) — ISBN 978-0-375-98859-2 (ebook)
[1. Sloths as pets. 2. Pets—Fiction.] I. Appelhans, Chris, illustrator. II. Title.
PZ7.O3277Sp 2013
[E]—dc23
2012047196

The text of this book was set in a font designed from the hand lettering of Chris Appelhans.
The illustrations were rendered in watercolor and pencil.
MANUFACTURED IN CHINA
10 8 6 4 3 5 7 9

First Edition

Sparky!

written by JENNY OFFILL

illustrated by CHRIS APPELHANS

schwartz & wade books · new york

I wanted a pet.

A bird or a bunny or a trained seal.

My mother said no to the bird.

No to the bunny.

No, no, no to the trained seal.

I asked her every day for a month, until she finally said,
"You can have any pet you want as long as it doesn't need
to be walked or bathed or fed."

I made her promise.

Then I went to see the school librarian.

Mrs. Kinklebaum (who knows everything in the world) pointed me to Volume S of the Animal Encyclopedia.

This is what I found:

SLOTH
(sláwth)

Sloths have been known to sleep more than sixteen hours a day. They sometimes hang upside down in trees, barely moving, for long periods of time.

They survive by eating leaves and drinking the dew that collects in them. It is said that sloths are the laziest animals in the world.

SNAKE
(snâyk)

My sloth arrived by Express Mail.

He was about the size of a mediumish dog, with a flat nose and a monkey face.

My mother wasn't happy, but a promise is a promise, I said.

Sparky, I decided. That will be your name.
I took him outside to his tree.

Sparky went right to sleep.

I made a sign and put it under the tree:

Guard Sloth!
Enter at
Your Own
Peril !!

It was two days

before I saw him awake.

He didn't know a lot of games, so I taught him some.
We played King of the Mountain

and I won.

We played Hide-and-Seek

and I won.

We played Kung Fu Fighter and I won.

We played Statue and Sparky
was very, very good.

That weekend, Mary Potts came over to investigate.

Let me show you what Mary Potts is like.

This is a picture of her room:

Before she even took off her coat, Mary said, "Let me see your new pet."

I had some worries, but I took her out to Sparky's tree. He opened his eyes and looked at us.

Then he closed them again.

I rubbed his belly, but it was too late.

We stood there for a while, watching him sleep. His fur
ruffled gently in the breeze.

"I feel sorry for you," Mary said. "My cat can dance on her hind legs. And my parrot knows twenty words, including *God* and *ice cream.*"

"Sparky knows tricks too," I told her. But she didn't believe me.

The next day, I made a poster and nailed it to the tree outside Mary Potts's house.

All week, we trained in secret.
Sometimes Sparky slept through
practice and I had to poke him awake.

Sometimes he forgot what he was
doing and we had to start over.

Sometimes he took so long to fetch that I went inside
and had dinner while I waited.

I was starting to think the poster had been a mistake.

But a promise is a promise.

On the day of the Trained Sloth
Extravaganza, my mother set up lawn chairs.

Three people came to see Sparky perform:
my mother, Mary Potts, and Mrs. Edwin, the
crossing guard.

(Mrs. Edwin approved of Sparky because he
never ran in the street.)

"Do I look like a ringmaster?" I asked my mother.

"You look very interesting," she told me.

I put a little glitter on Sparky just before the curtain went up.

I kept wishing I had written *Two Tricks* on the poster, instead of *Countless Tricks*.

"Play dead, Sparky!" I said, and he did.

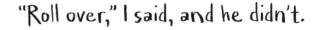

"Roll over," I said, and he didn't.

"Speak!" I commanded.

We all waited.

And waited.

"Speak?" I said.

Sparky looked at me. The only thing you could hear was the wind in the trees.

"He has a very pretty coat, doesn't he?" Mrs. Edwin said finally.

"You can't just invent a brand-new pet like that,"
Mary told me. "A pet no one's ever even had!"

My mother came out with lemonade and cookies,
but everyone said they had to be going.

Sparky and I watched them; then my mother
made me put the chairs away.

Afterward, I gave Sparky a cookie, but he ate
it so slowly that I took it back again.

It was getting dark out. I looked at him and he looked at me.

You could hear all the neighborhood dogs barking.

I reached over and tagged him on his claw.

"You're it, Sparky," I said.
And for a long, long time he was.